Special thanks to Sarah Hawkins

ORCHARD BOOKS

First published in 2017 by The Watts Publishing Group

1 3 5 7 9 10 8 6 4 2

A CIP catalogue record for this book is available from the British Library.

ISBN 978 1 40834 749 2

Printed and bound in China

The paper and board used in this book are made from wood from responsible sources.

Orchard Books
An imprint of Hachette Children's Group
Part of The Watts Publishing Group Limited
Carmelite House, 50 Victoria Embankment, London EC4Y 0DZ

An Hachette UK Company
www.hachette.co.uk
www.hachettechildrens.co.uk

The Movie Storybook

ORCHARD

Princess
Twilight
Sparkle

Tempest

Princess Skystar

Queen Novo

Capper

Captain Celano

The Storm King

Storm Creatures

Contents

✶ ✶ ✶

Part One: The Friendship Festival

Part Two: Pirate Adventures

Part Three: Seaponies!

Part One
The Friendship Festival

Chapter One
Princess Planning

Twilight Sparkle was in Canterlot Castle. Sometimes she could not believe that she was really a princess. She loved being the Princess of Friendship and doing magic with all her best friends.

But today, Princess Twilight was feeling very nervous. She had to organise the Friendship Festival, and everyone was counting on her to make it a success! Ponies were coming from all over Equestria.

Twilight really wanted everyone to have lots of fun. But before the guests arrived, she had to show her party plans to Princess Celestia, Princess Luna and Princess Cadance.

Her dragon assistant, Spike, came to help her. They told the other princesses about her ideas for the party.

Twilight asked Princess Celestia, Princess Luna and Princess Cadance to help her make a beautiful, magical light show at the end of the festival.

But the princesses reminded Twilight that she had all the magic she needed. They told her to ask her friends for help!

Chapter Two
Party Chaos

All of Twilight Sparkle's friends had gathered at Canterlot Castle.

"Yippeeee!" Pinkie Pie shouted, bouncing up and down. She was very excited about helping with the party.

Pinkie Pie loved planning
parties!

Rainbow Dash, Fluttershy,
Applejack and Rarity were
there too. Twilight gave them
all jobs. Pinkie Pie was in
charge of the party decorations.

Rarity made everything shine with beautiful jewels.

Applejack had brought some delicious apple juice for everyone to share.

Fluttershy was in charge of the music. A famous singer

called Songbird Serenade was going to sing at the festival. Fluttershy was training a choir of birds to sing with her.

Soon the friends were all busy with their tasks. They had to get everything ready!

Twilight ran from one friend
to another, trying to make sure
that they were doing things
properly.

"Everything has to be
absolutely perfect!" Twilight
Sparkle told them.

But as she interrupted her friends, they started making mistakes. Pinkie Pie's balloon escaped and floated towards Fluttershy. The balloon flew into Fluttershy's bird chorus and scared them away!

At the same time, Rainbow Dash tried to help Rarity to decorate. The speedy pony finished the job very quickly, but it was a big mess!

Twilight Sparkle looked around in dismay. What were they going to do?

Chapter Three
Working Together

Pinkie Pie saw that her friend was upset. She went over to Twilight Sparkle and gave her a great big hug. "We can fix this, as long as we work together," she told Twilight Sparkle.

Twilight felt better. Then Pinkie Pie set off a party cannon and covered Twilight with cake!

At that exact moment, Songbird Serenade, the famous singer, suddenly appeared!

Twilight welcomed her to the festival.

But Songbird wasn't the only pony who had just arrived. Storm clouds appeared in the sky as a big ship arrived. A Unicorn with a broken horn marched into the palace. It was Tempest.

Twilight Sparkle and the other princesses said, "Welcome to the Festival of Friendship!"

But Tempest had not come to make friends. "Give me your magic," she told the princesses.

"Or we will take over Equestria!"

The princesses fought Tempest and the Storm Creatures. Tempest threw green magic at the princesses and turned them to stone!

Princess Celestia told Princess Luna to get help. "Go and get help from the Queen of the Hippo—" she began, but then Tempest turned her and Luna to stone. Twilight was the only princess left!

Rainbow Dash helped Twilight Sparkle escape. The ponies escaped from the Storm Creatures by jumping down a waterfall. The six brave ponies and Spike had to work together again. This time they had to save Equestria!

Part Two
Pirate Adventures

Chapter Four

A Strange Land

The ponies climbed out of the waterfall and looked around. They were all upset.

"I have to find the Queen of the Hippos and save Equestria," Twilight Sparkle said. Twilight did not want her friends to come with her. She thought it was too dangerous.

Rainbow Dash, Fluttershy, Rarity, Applejack, Pinkie Pie and Spike told Twilight that they were coming with her. They were her friends. They set off together to find the queen.

At the same time, Tempest was with her master, the Storm King.

"If you take over Equestria, I will fix your horn," the Storm King told her. Tempest just had to capture the last princess …

"I'll get Princess Twilight Sparkle," Tempest promised. "And turn her to stone!"

Chapter Five

A New Friend

The ponies were lost in a
strange land. Everything there
was very big and the creatures
were very strange. They met a
cat called Capper, who said he
could help them. He took them
to his house and gave them tea.

It was very warm and cosy, but Twilight Sparkle felt like there was something wrong.

The other ponies all relaxed. "Darling, look at your coat, it is all torn!" Rarity said to Capper. She started to fix

Capper's coat for him.

Twilight went to Capper's library to see if she could find out about the Hippos. Suddenly, she found something. "Hippogriffs, not Hippos!" she told the others when she came back. "Princess Celestia was trying to tell us to find the Hippogriffs. They are ponies that live at the very top of Mount Aris."

"Then that is where we need to go!" Rainbow Dash said excitedly.

As the ponies celebrated,
there was a knock at the door.
It was Tempest!

The ponies sneaked out the
back door. "Where are they?"
Tempest asked. Capper looked
down at his new coat. The
ponies had been so kind to him.

"That way," he told Tempest, but he pointed the wrong way!

The ponies had escaped from Tempest again!

Chapter Six
Pirates

The ponies sneaked aboard a flying ship. The ponies hid, but the crew found them.

The captain was called Captain Celano. Captain Celano explained that they used to be pirates, but now

they just delivered parcels for
Tempest and her wicked boss,
the Storm King.

   They were not very scary.
Rainbow Dash was very
disappointed. Pirates are meant
to be fierce!

Rainbow Dash said that they should stop working for the Storm King. She sang them a song about being awesome.

"Yeah!" the pirates agreed.

"We are not working for the Storm King any more!"

Captain Celano declared.

The ponies and the pirates all celebrated.

Rainbow Dash was so happy that she flew over the ship really fast. She flew so fast that she made a Sonic Rainboom!

Tempest saw the Sonic Rainboom in the sky. She and the Storm Creatures raced to the pirate ship!

"Where is Twilight Sparkle?" Tempest asked.

The pirates helped the ponies

to hide from Tempest, just
in time. The ponies escaped
through a hole in the bottom
of the ship. For a second, they
were falling!

Then Twilight quickly used
her magic to save her friends.

Twilight made a beautiful hot-air balloon appear. Spike used his fire breath to heat the air and make the hot-air balloon fly.

As they flew away, they saw a mountain in the distance.

They were on their way to Mount Aris to find the Queen of the Hippogriffs!

Part Three
Seaponies!

Chapter Seven

Mount Aris

The ponies arrived at Mount
Aris, but there was no one
there.

"Hello!" Pinkie Pie called,
but no one answered.

Just then, they heard a voice
singing far away. They ran

towards the sound of the voice. They followed it to a beautiful fountain. There was a creature there, but as they ran towards her, she dived into the water!

"Wait!" Twilight called. But it was too late.

"CANNONBALL!" Pinkie
Pie yelled, jumping into the
fountain with an enormous
splash.

Her friends all quickly
jumped in after her. They were
sucked into a whirlpool, which

swirled them around and
around.

"Wheeeeeeee!" yelled Pinkie
Pie excitedly.

The ponies were deep
underwater. Suddenly
they found that they were
wearing magical bubble
helmets! Twilight Sparkle
and her friends swam around
underwater with their magical
bubble helmets on. It was fun!

Then a beautiful seahorse
appeared. "My name is Princess
Skystar," she told them.

Princess Skystar was very friendly. The ponies explained that they needed to find the Hippogriffs. Princess Skystar took them to her beautiful Seapony kingdom!

Chapter Eight

Queen Novo

Princess Skystar's mum was called Queen Novo. She was not pleased that Princess Skystar had brought the ponies to their underwater kingdom.

Twilight Sparkle explained what had happened.

"We need to find the queen of the Hippogriffs," Twilight Sparkle said.

"That is me," Queen Novo told them. The ponies were amazed.

Queen Novo explained that years ago the Hippogriffs

had used a magic pearl to become Seaponies. She showed them the pearl. Suddenly all the ponies found that they had beautiful Seapony tails. Spike was transformed into a pufferfish! They all swam around in excitement.

But while the ponies were playing with Princess Skystar, Twilight Sparkle tried to steal the magic pearl. The other ponies were very shocked. Stealing is wrong!

Twilight was very sorry. She thought the magic pearl could save Equestria.

The other ponies were cross with Twilight. But when they left her alone, Tempest found her …

"Tempest has taken Twilight!" Spike told the other ponies.

They were all upset. Princess Skystar promised to help. She left the water and her Seapony tail turned back into legs.

She promised to help save Twilight Sparkle, and Equestria.

"We will help!" came a voice from a ship. It was Capper and the pirates!

Everyone got on board and they flew back to Equestria.

Chapter Nine

A Happy Ending

As they travelled back to
Canterlot, the friends made
a plan. When they got there,
some of them pulled an
enormous cake into the castle.
Then the ponies and pirates
burst out of the cake and

started to fight the Storm
Creatures.

"Remember you promised
to fix my horn," Tempest told
the Storm King. But the Storm
King just laughed. He was
never going to fix her horn.

Tempest had been tricked!

The Storm King made a huge tornado. Tempest was sucked inside, but Twilight saved her.

Pinkie Pie, Rarity and all the other ponies arrived. "I'm sorry I tried to steal," Twilight said.

The ponies all forgave her, but the Storm King tried to turn them all to stone!

Tempest stopped him, but she was turned to stone instead. The ponies managed to get the Storm King's staff. The Storm

King was defeated!

The princesses and Tempest turned back to normal again. The princesses gathered around Twilight Sparkle.

"You saved the kingdom!" said Princess Celestia.

"With help from my old friends and my new friends," Twilight said. "You should stay in Equestria," she told Tempest.

Tempest was feeling sad about her broken horn.

"Your horn is perfect just the way it is," Twilight told her.

"Thank you!" Tempest used her broken horn to shoot fireworks up into the sky.

"Amazing, Tempest!" everyone cried.

"My real name is Fizzlepop Berrytwist," Tempest said shyly.

The ponies all welcomed
Fizzlepop to Equestria.
Songbird Serenade started
singing. Twilight looked at
her friends happily. "This is
going to be the best Friendship
Festival ever!" she said.

There's lots of colouring, sticker and activity fun with My Little Pony!